As everyone knows, the North Pole is up here....

And Santa circles the globe .... just to be clear.

Magic Christmas Pajamas

MARY RIEDINGER

Copyright © 2021 Mary Riedinger
All rights reserved.
ISBN: 9798465887335

Which means, every Christmas before making his rounds, he flies over your house without making a sound.

On our side of the world, all are awake
and still cruising, but down under and over,
the children are snoozing.

So that's where he's heading, far far away,

where the children are sleeping,

they've finished their day.

Yes, him and his reindeer and his magical sled,

glide silently above, right over your head...

But you're still awake, the sun hasn't set, it's

Christmas Eve! Santas coming! You're excited I bet!

And here is a secret that very few know ...As he flies up above he tosses a gift down below.

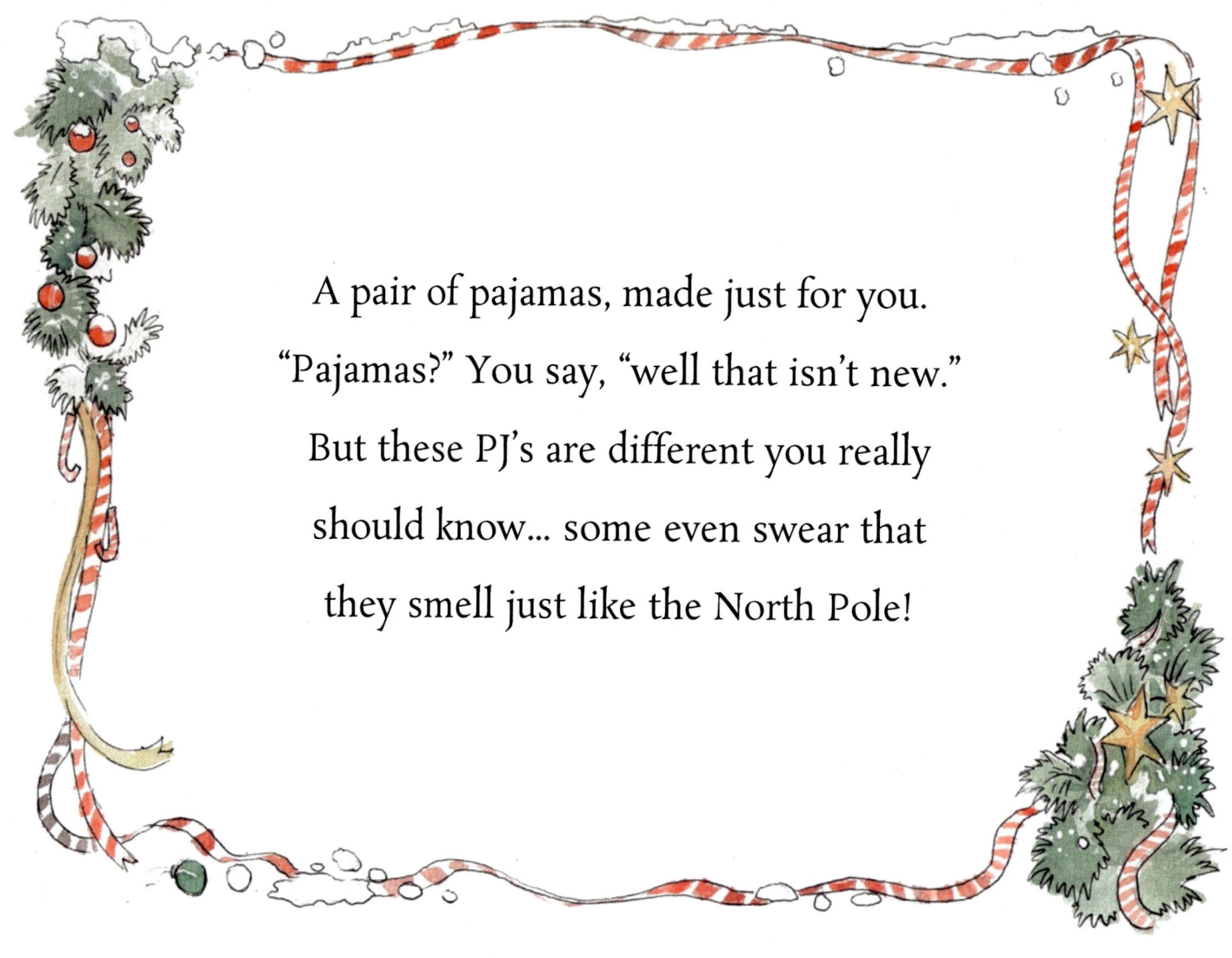

A pair of pajamas, made just for you.
"Pajamas?" You say, "well that isn't new."
But these PJ's are different you really
should know... some even swear that
they smell just like the North Pole!

So, on Christmas Eve, as your nights winding down, look outside before bed to see what might be found.

Directly from Santa, a package for you, check the roof, and the porch and in the trees too!

Sometimes it can be tricky to find in the yard, dropping gifts from a sled can be sorta hard.

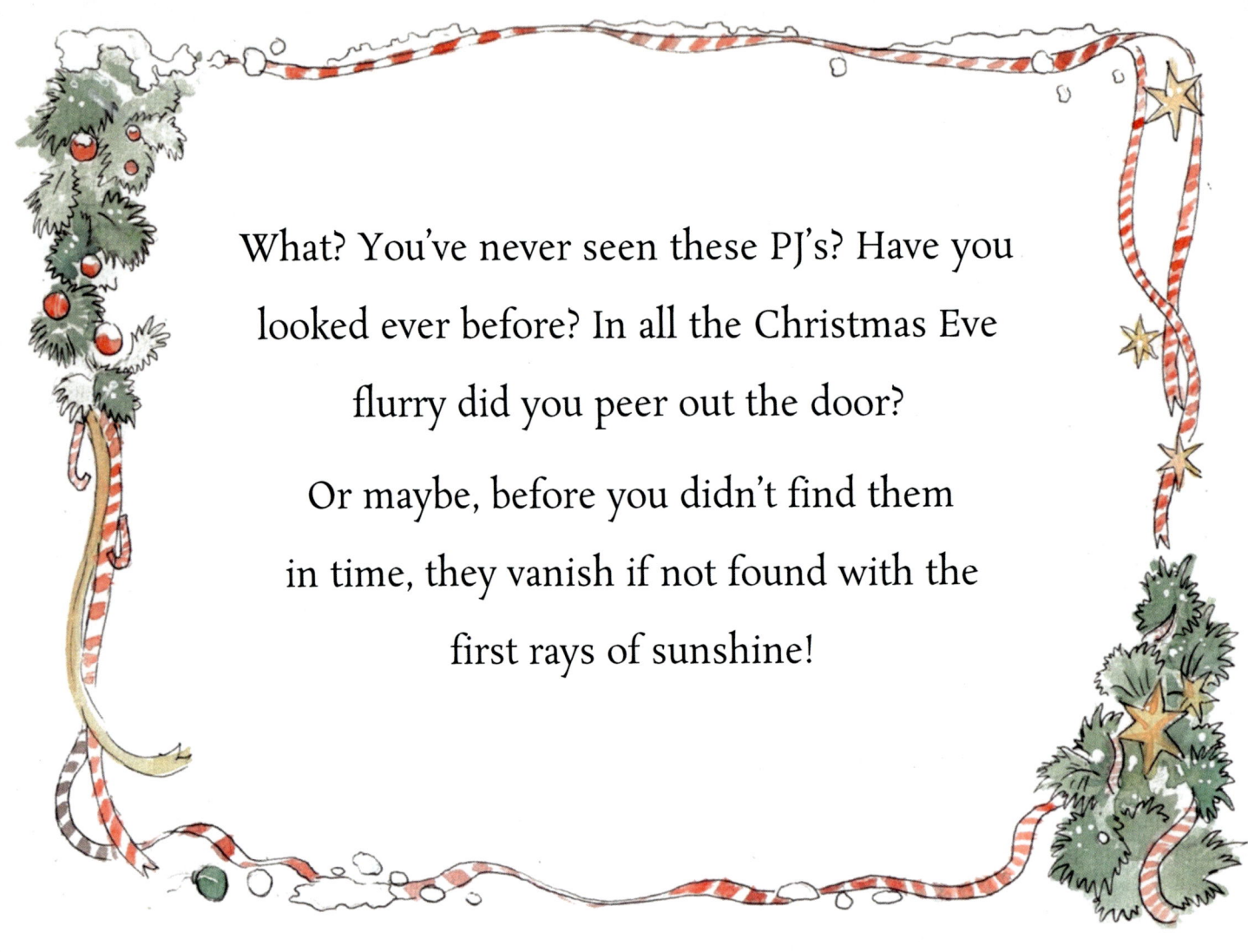

What? You've never seen these PJ's? Have you looked ever before? In all the Christmas Eve flurry did you peer out the door?

Or maybe, before you didn't find them in time, they vanish if not found with the first rays of sunshine!

When they are found, put them on with delight, feel the enchantment surround you on this magical night!

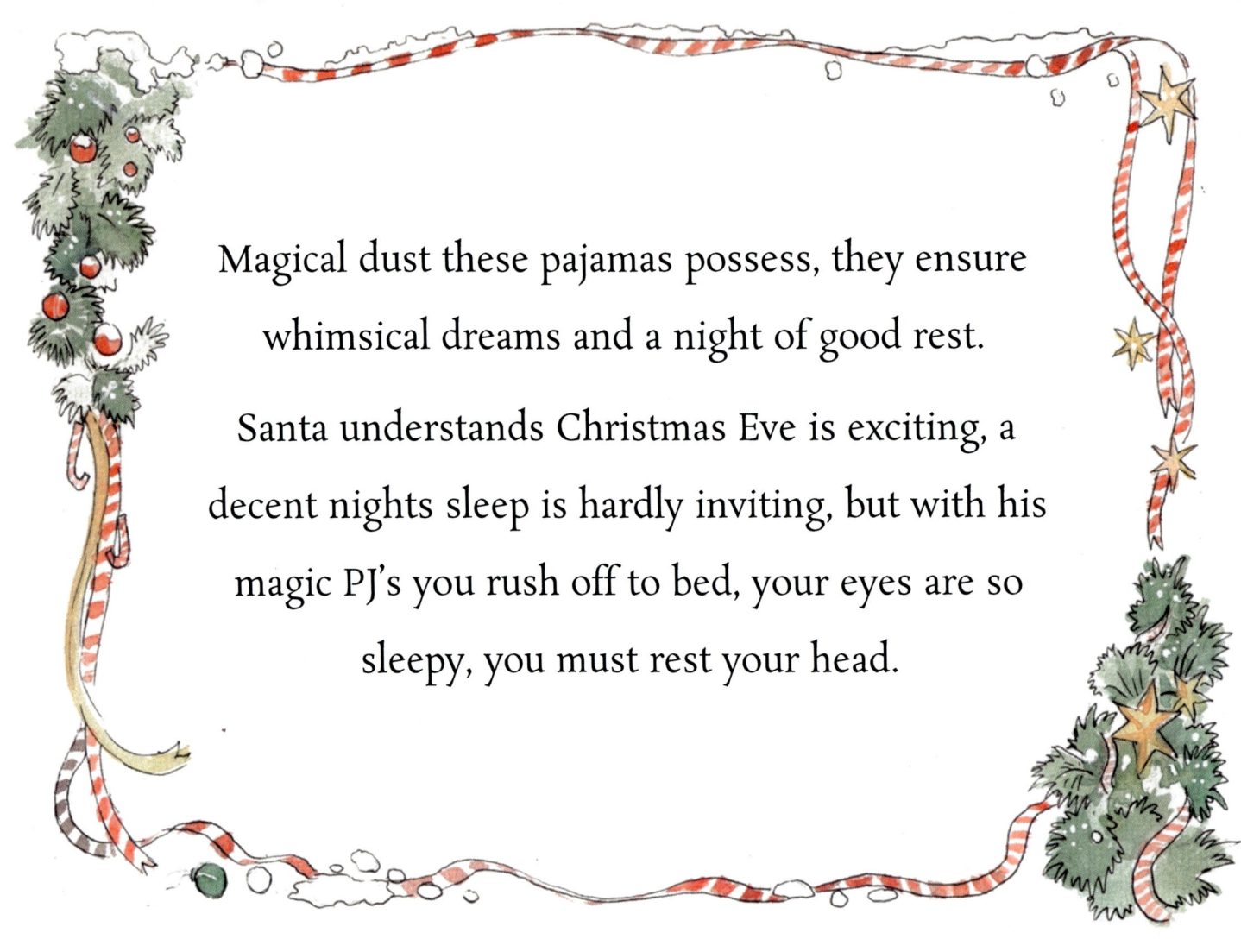

Magical dust these pajamas possess, they ensure whimsical dreams and a night of good rest.

Santa understands Christmas Eve is exciting, a decent nights sleep is hardly inviting, but with his magic PJ's you rush off to bed, your eyes are so sleepy, you must rest your head.

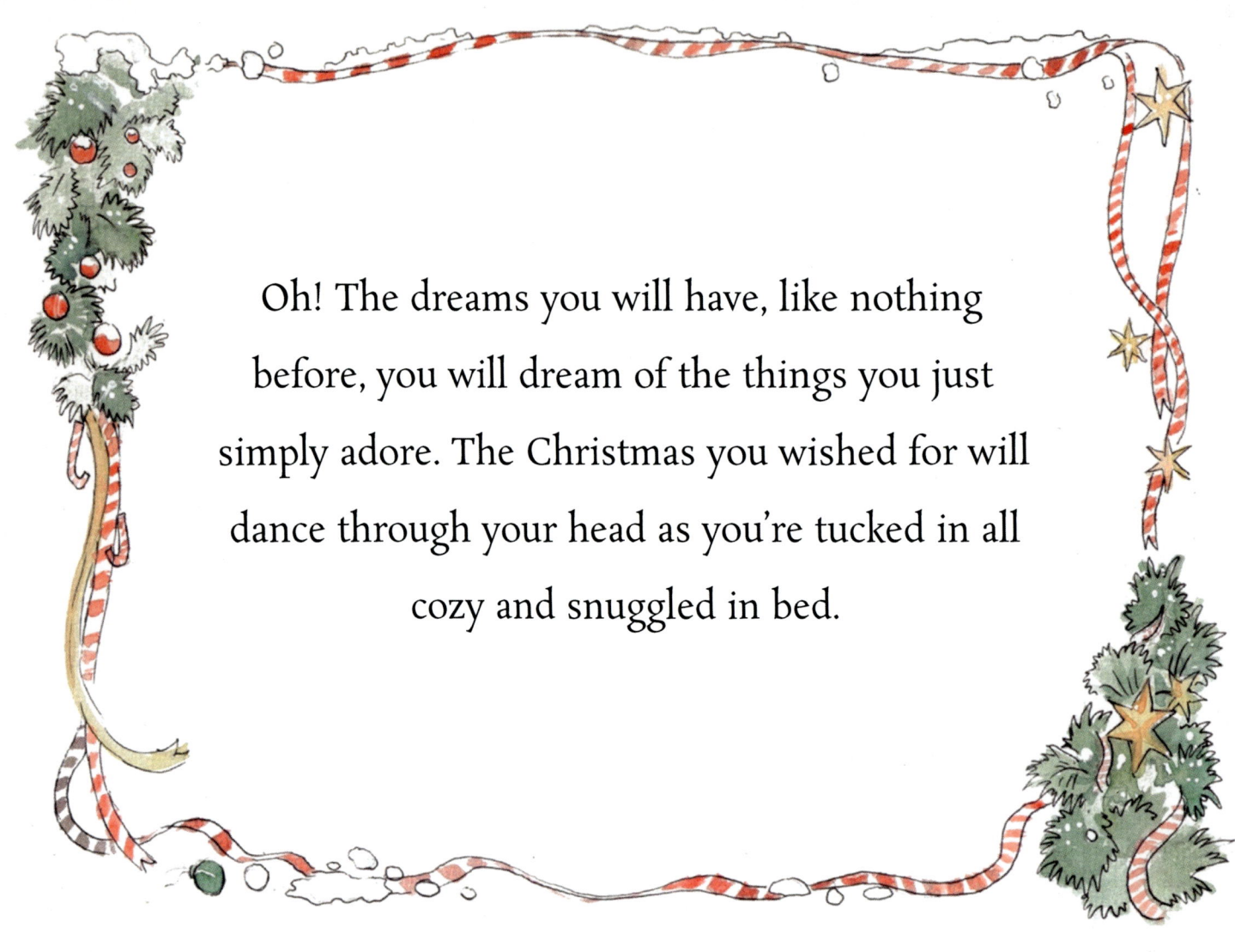

Oh! The dreams you will have, like nothing before, you will dream of the things you just simply adore. The Christmas you wished for will dance through your head as you're tucked in all cozy and snuggled in bed.

Oh, one last thing, Santa does keep his list, so remember only good boys and girls get his Christmas Eve gift.

Made in the USA
Middletown, DE
17 October 2021